"Grammy, I only said one teeny little thing today at recess, and now everybody thinks I'm some kind of criminal."

"What did you say, Tabitha?"

"Well, the boys were arguing with the Queen about whether the cops beat up on people, like on TV. All I said was they weren't mean to me when I was arrested."

Grammy gulped her tea. "Tabitha, you weren't arrested! Arrested means you are charged with a crime. That is absolutely not why you were at the police station. Maybe you should just tell them the whole story and be done with it."

I was concentrating on my tea. "Never, Grammy. It's too embarrassing! It's easier just to let them think I'm a criminal."

Be sure to read all the books
in the Tabitha Sarah Bigbee series:

Pickle Stew
Gorilla on the Midway
Big Mouth

Big Mouth

A TABITHA SARAH BIGBEE BOOK

BY WENDY LORD

Chariot Books
A Division of Cook Communications

IT'S A
FLIP
BOOK!

Chariot Books™ is an imprint of David C. Cook Publishing Co.
David C. Cook Publishing Co., Elgin, Illinois 60120
David C. Cook Publishing Co., Weston, Ontario
Nova Distribution Ltd., Eastbourne, England

BIG MOUTH
© 1994 by Wendy Lord

Designed by Cheryl Blum
Cover illustration by Paul Casale
Internal illustrations by Kate Flanagan
First Printing, 1994
Printed in the United States of America
98 97 96 95 94   5 4 3 2 1

Library of Congress Cataloging-in-Publication Data
Lord, Wendy.
Big mouth / by Wendy Lord.
p.   cm. — (Tabitha series ; 3rd)
Summary: When rumors start circulating at school that Tabitha was
arrested for drug-related activities, she finds that with Jesus' help, she
can confront the lies and get on with her life.
ISBN 0-7814-0084-8
[1. Gossip—Fiction. 2. Schools—Fiction. 3. Christian life—Fiction.] I.
Title. II. Series: Lord, Wendy. Tabitha series; 3rd.
PZ7.L8785Bi 1994
[Fic]—dc20   94-1799
                                                                CIP AC

• •

To
Erica and Emilee
This book would not have been possible
without your field research. Thanks.
I love you.

Set a guard over my mouth, O Lord;
keep watch over the door of my lips.

Psalm 141:3

Contents

Chapter 1   A Slip of the Lip   9

Chapter 2   Criminal Baby Liar   21

Chapter 3   Fifty Different Stories   31

Chapter 4   The Dealer   43

Chapter 5   Tied Up in Knots   53

Chapter 6   Proof Positive   61

Chapter 7   Jason's Big Mouth   69

Chapter 8   The Sinking Ship   77

Chapter 9   The Truth   89

Chapter 10   Free Indeed   99

A Slip of the Lip

My name is Tabitha Sarah Bigbee and I have a big mouth. I also have Mrs. Goodman again.

I didn't flunk. Mrs. Goodman got promoted up a grade. She said she needed a change, but it didn't work because most of us are in her class again.

I don't mind. I really like Mrs. Goodman. It's just that in our school, there are only two or three classes for each grade. They divide up the kids alphabetically, so the same kids are in my class almost every year. Now I have the same teacher, too!

Jason, who lives next door to me, is in my class again, of course. His name is

Harrington, and H is pretty close to B for Bigbee, which is me. There's always hope, though, that about fifty new kids will move to our town and their names will all start with D or E, and then Jason H will be shoved into the next class. But not this year.

Also, "Queen Kirsten and her Court" are all in my class. Kirsten's last name is Bingham. That is just too close to Bigbee to ever hope for relief. The girls in her court change constantly, depending on who wants to obey her every command, or who she happens to be mad at, or who just got a new anything and is willing to lend it—or give it—to the Queen.

No one calls her the Queen but me, and I never do out loud, except to Grammy. If I called her the Queen to her face, it would be asking for more trouble than I usually get from her. I have only been in her court a few times, like when I first met her and invited her to my birthday party, or once when I brought a huge bag of M&M's to school.

Grammy says that to have a friend, you have to be friendly, but we've both agreed that it doesn't always work. We've pretty much tried everything in the last few years to get the girls in my class to be my friends. They are for awhile—as long as it suits them or until Queen Kirsten tells them not to be. At least I do have Kelly and Sara. We always jump rope. Every recess. We're just about the best in the school. The Queen says jumping rope is for boring babies, and she stays away.

Well, I may be boring, but my big mouth has provided the school with a whole lot of excitement.

It all started when I spent the week before Labor Day at the fair with my new non-best friend, Sonya. We had entered our rabbits in the exhibition, but we spent most of our time trying to win a prize at one of the game booths. The week started out bad,

11

got worse, and ended up horrible.

It was so awful that once we got home, I promised myself I was not going to think about it anymore. I was never going to say a word about it to anyone, especially after having to tell it all in detail to the police.

Well, at recess on the very first day of school, I broke that promise. Queen Kirsten reigned over the playground as usual and had her court around her. They were arguing with Jason and some of the boys. I went over to find out what was going on.

I heard Jason say, "They do too! My dad's a lawyer, and he knows all the cops."

Someone else said, "Yeah, and if you don't confess, they shove you around until you do!"

A couple of girls stomped away.

The Queen announced, "You guys watch too much TV. You don't know anything about the real police. Nobody gets beat up for not confessing."

"Oh, and how would you know? How many times have you been hauled in by the police?"

Kirsten was red-faced and getting angry. "I just know, that's all. I've never seen the inside of a police station. But I wouldn't be surprised if you guys spend every weekend in jail. You deserve to get beat up by the police."

I don't know why I said what I said next. Maybe I thought if I stuck up for Kirsten, she'd leave me alone for awhile. Or maybe I just knew the boys were wrong.

"Kirsten's right," I said. "They weren't mean to me when I got arrested."

Great. In the split second of silence that followed, I thought of a thousand reasons why I shouldn't have said that. Why couldn't I just let them have their stupid argument without me? I knew the very next question would be "What did you get arrested for?" and I didn't want to answer that!

"What did you get arrested for, Tabitha?"
There it was.

"Nothing. Never mind. And anyway, the whole night I was there, I didn't see one person get shoved around. I never even saw anyone in handcuffs." But it was no good. The conversation wasn't about the police anymore. It was about me!

"People don't spend the night in jail for

14

nothing, Tabitha. What did you do?"

"I wasn't in jail!" I hollered. "And I didn't spend the night!"

Then the bell rang to go in. We ran to line up at the door and Sara slid in behind me. "Tell me what you did, Tabitha. I won't tell anybody."

"Sara, just forget it."

"My sister got arrested for shoplifting once," she whispered. "They caught her with the stuff. She's got a record and everything."

"Sara, I wasn't shoplifting, and I didn't . . ."

Just then we passed through the door into the hall. We aren't allowed to say a word once we come inside. Mrs. Goodman caught my eye and I shut up.

Back at my desk, I looked over at Sara. She winked at me and smiled a knowing little smile. She really did think I was a shoplifter.

15

After school, I went right in to find Grammy.

Grammy is the one I talk to. We've always lived with her—ever since I was born. Mom and Dad are great, but it's easier to talk to Grammy. And now that she has a broken leg, she has more time to sit around and talk.

The kettle of water was on the stove, and Grammy was at the kitchen table reading her Bible. Her cast was propped up on another chair.

"Your toes are looking pretty good, Grammy. They're not as purple as they were when you first came home."

Grammy put her Bible aside and pulled out a chair for me.

"How's Androcles doing, Tabitha? Is she glad to be back home from the fair?"

"I haven't checked on her since this morning. But oh, Grammy, you should have seen her when we first got home. She raced around and around in circles, sniffing like a

16

puppy. I guess she was checking to see if there were any other rabbits around."

Gram chuckled. "Being at the fair must have been a strange experience for her."

"With her silky red fur, she was the finest rabbit there. I think she knew it too. I got her home just in time, before she got conceited."

Grammy got up to make us our after-school cup of tea. "Cranberry, Tabitha?"

"Yep! It's always cranberry. Just the smell of it makes me feel safe."

Grammy put her hand on my shoulder. "Are you having trouble feeling safe, Tabitha?"

"No," I said to Grammy. *Yes!* I said to myself. I think about that awful man practically every minute. I promised myself I wouldn't think about him, or ever talk about him, but I had already opened my big mouth at school. And it was only the first day!

"Tabitha, honey, I think it will help to

17

talk about what happened at the fair. It's going to take awhile to get over it."

I bounced my tea bag up and down in the water. "No, Grammy, talking only makes it worse. I only said one teeny little thing today at recess, and now everybody thinks I'm some kind of criminal."

"What did you say, Tabitha?"

"Well, the boys were arguing with the Queen about whether the cops beat up on people, like on TV. All I said was they weren't mean to me when I was arrested."

Grammy gulped her tea. "Tabitha, you weren't arrested! Arrested means you are charged with a crime. That is absolutely not why you were at the police station. Maybe you should just tell them the whole story and be done with it."

I was concentrating on my tea. "Never, Grammy. The whole thing is too embarrassing! They've been preaching Stranger Awareness to us since kindergarten, so what do I do? The first chance I get, I

18

practically skip right up to the grossest guy at the fair. How stupid can you get!"

Grammy just sipped her tea and didn't say anything. I finished mine and got up to rinse the cup.

"No, Grammy," I said. "It's easier just to let them think I'm a criminal."

2

Criminal Baby Liar

When the Queen saw me coming across the playground the next morning, she turned to face me. She waved her arm at her court, and they all fell into place behind her.

She stood with her hands on her hips, blocking my path. "All right, Bigbee! Tell us what you did. Otherwise you're going to get yourself a pretty bad reputation."

"Just leave me alone. I didn't do anything."

"Then you're a dirty liar as well as a criminal. We don't like baby girls who lie, do we?"

The other girls shook their heads and sneered at me. I tried to shove past her, but she grabbed my arm.

"Put your right hand on your baby jump rope and repeat after me. . . ." I yanked free and ran while she chanted, ". . . I swear to tell the truth, the whole truth and nothing but the truth, so help me God."

So help me God. Kirsten didn't know it, but she was right about that part. I wonder if Jesus gets tired of me asking for help. Grammy says not, but it's hard to imagine.

Well, I put a ton of energy into jumping rope with Sara and Kelly for the rest of the recess. Even if I was a criminal baby liar without a best friend, at least I always had someone to jump rope with. And when it was my turn to crank the rope, I counted out loud so I wouldn't think about anything else. And I didn't look at Kirsten and her court even once.

When I got home from school, Grammy had my cranberry tea all ready.

"Well, hi there. What are your plans for this gorgeous afternoon?"

I hung my backpack on a hook and pulled out a chair. "I'd like to go down to Jason's to practice. Have you seen my helmet and pads?"

"They're out on the porch," Grammy

23

said. "Are you getting any good?"

I stirred some honey into my tea, and watched while it swirled around and dissolved.

"I guess skateboarding isn't any different than jumping rope."

Mom came into the kitchen and reached for a cup. "How's that, sweetie?"

"Well, it is different, but I mean you have to have good balance. Maybe I'll get good someday."

Mom sat down with us. "I hear you're the school champ at jump rope."

I shrugged. "Kelly holds the record for Red Hot Pepper, but no one can jump on one foot as long as I can. My tops is 91 on my right foot and 63 on my left foot."

Grammy whistled. "That's pretty good!"

Mom inspected the underside of my chin. "That's almost healed up! Jumping rope has got to be easier on your chin than skateboarding! Try to keep all your body parts in one piece from now on, okay?"

I finished my snack and headed for Jason's house where I found him sitting in a heap at the bottom of his ramp.

The ramp looks like the valley between two mountains, except the mountains are only about four or five feet high. Jason and I are working on getting from the platform at the top of one side to the platform on the other.

The trick, we discovered, is to just rock back and forth in the curved bottom until you're really comfortable. You have to get the feel of pumping your legs and just how far up the other side each effort will take you.

Then you can try taking off from one platform, racing down the valley, and seeing if you can make it to the other platform without killing yourself.

Jason had obviously been practicing while I was at the fair, because he looked pretty good.

But neither one of us felt very energetic an

hour later after we had rocked back and forth nine million times.

We sat down on the grass. "My legs are never going to get used to this," I moaned. "Maybe I'll just sit here for about a week."

Jason laid out flat on the ground. "Me too. But only till Friday night. I'd rather not be here when Dad mows the grass this weekend."

Then he sat up and said, "You'd better watch out for Kirsten. She says she has proof."

"Proof of what, Jason?"

"Proof of what you did."

"I didn't do anything! What can she have proof of?"

"Well, first she said her uncle caught someone stealing from his video store last week, and she was going to find out if it was you. So I told her it couldn't have been you, 'cause you were at the fair all week.

"Then she started to laugh, and said, 'Oh, so that's it! Well, I can certainly get

26

proof of that easy enough!' "

I took off my helmet and stared at Jason. He just stared right back.

"I gotta get home," I said, and struggled to my feet.

I picked up my board and started down the driveway, but Jason called after me, "I'm telling you Tabitha, she knows something. Watch out."

When I got home, supper was ready. Grammy's chicken pie was so good, even my sore muscles started to feel better.

But halfway through the meal I began to wonder if my Grammy was going crazy!

While we were eating she said, "You all know every fall I send packages to the Mexican outreach."

"Yeah, Grammy. When are we going to start? I like to help you with that."

Before Gram could answer, Mom said, "I'm a step ahead of you! I've already got

27

four little dresses made. They're so easy and quick, compared to making wedding gowns anyway. And I'm saving scraps, so Tabitha can make some knot dolls."

Daddy looked confused. "If they're not dolls, what are they?"

"No, Daddy! Not 'Not Dolls.' 'Knot Dolls'! You know, K-N-O-T! Last year in social studies we learned about them.

"Colonial girls made them out of of scraps of cloth. They didn't use any thread, because thread was so expensive and hard to get back then, so they tied the dolls in knots. They were small enough to hold in your hand, and they had dresses and aprons and even little scarves on their heads.

"The book said kids were allowed to take them to church because they didn't make any noise when they dropped them."

Daddy laughed. "Hey, now there's an idea! You could make one for Robbie Thompson to bring to church. Then maybe he'd leave his Leggos at home."

"Well," Grammy said. And then she waited until we were all looking at her. "This year, I thought I'd just take the things to Mexico myself."

3

Fifty Different Stories

Daddy stopped the fork halfway to his mouth and stared at his mother.

Grammy straightened up in her chair and served herself some salad. "Don't look at me like that Richard. I've been thinking this over for a long time, and I've been in touch with the ministry there. They always need extra volunteers."

"Mom!" said Daddy. "How will we pay for a trip to Mexico? And how long will you be gone? You're still in a cast, for crying out loud."

"My leg will be fine by Christmas. And it won't cost as much as you think. Maybe just airfare. They put everyone up in some kind of dormitory and serve the meals all together. If nothing else, I can at least wash dishes!"

Suddenly it struck me. "Grammy, you can't leave at Christmas! You can't! You have to be here, with us!"

Grammy pushed her plate aside. "Well I didn't say I was going for sure, and I don't know all the details. Let's not talk about it any more now. I just thought I'd give you all some time to get used to the idea."

She struggled up from her chair and got her crutches.

"Excuse me. I'm going to go lie down."

After she left, I just sat there. I haven't had much appetite lately anyway, but now there was no way I could eat.

When Mom and Dad were finished eating, Mom started clearing the table. Always, except for when she was in the hospital, Grammy and I do dishes. Mom

32

usually goes to work at her sewing machine.

But Mom and Daddy did the dishes. I sat in the living room staring at the door of the downstairs guest room. That's where Grammy is sleeping while her leg heals.

Even our dog, Everett, was acting weird. He was lying outside her room with his head on his paws, just staring at the crack under the door.

I tried to figure out why she was acting this way. She was always a very regular grammy before. Maybe she broke more than her leg when she fell off the porch. I think it affected her mind.

". . . at her age!" said my father.

". . . just the point!" said my mother. "If she wants to do something different, or important, or even foolish, at her age, we should support her."

Daddy mumbled something I couldn't really hear about money from selling the potato house.

33

"You're right," Mom said. "We did say we'd put the money back into the property. And we've done that with the new porch. You have plenty set aside for any other repairs we'll need. But really, Richard, it was hers and her father's before it was ours. A few hundred dollars isn't unreasonable."

Daddy sat down at the table and put his head in his hands.

Mom rubbed his shoulders. "This isn't about the money at all, is it?"

Daddy sighed. "No, I guess it isn't. I guess I just want my mother to always be the way she always was. This crazy idea of hers is so . . . oh, I don't know. I guess I reacted before I thought about what was fair. I'd better go apologize."

"Well, it's not fair," I said.

They looked up quickly. I guess they hadn't realized I could hear them from where I was sitting.

"It's not! If Grammy leaves at Christmas, it'll ruin everything."

34

They came out and sat on the sofa with me. "Whose life is she living, Tabitha?" Daddy asked. "Hers or ours?"

"Well of course it's her own life, but . . ."

"Then until we know more about it, and why she wants to go, we'll just leave it alone, okay?"

Mom knocked softly on Grammy's door, and when there was no answer, she pushed it open. Grammy was tucked in bed and sound asleep.

"You'll have to make your apologies in the morning, Richard," Mom whispered.

"Why do you have to apologize, Daddy?" I asked.

He shook his head a little. "Well, for treating her like a child, for one thing. But mostly for not hearing her out before I started objecting to it."

Grammy always tells me that God can make something good out of even the worst

situation. So far, the only good that's come out of Grammy's news is that I got through a whole night without thinking about that disgusting man at the fair, or what people were saying about me at school.

But when I got off the bus the next morning, the Queen was right there waiting for me.

"I know what you did, Bigbee. No wonder you were arrested. I hope they put you in jail till you graduate. Don't think that anyone is going to hang out with you—ever."

She flounced away, followed by a bigger court than usual.

I just stood there trying to understand what she was talking about. It didn't take long. I heard it fifty times in fifty different versions before the bell even rang for school to start.

I think the only true part was that Kirsten's grandfather is the racing commissioner for the fair. He just happened to be somewhere near the security office when the police pulled up to get that man.

Beyond that the story gets really garbled. It seems that everybody figures he was being arrested for drugs, since that's the usual thing. But the details change every time someone tells it.

How I get into the story is amazing! Andy says Kirsten's grandfather saw the man selling me drugs. Terry says it was Kirsten's uncle who saw me buying drugs from him. Jason says he heard from Chris that I had somebody beat the guy up because he didn't pay.

Boy, oh, boy! Now I'm not only a criminal baby liar, but I'm also a druggie with a hit man at my command. WOW!

Math, of course, was impossible. I couldn't even read the numbers on the page, much less multiply them. Everyone hates me, and now I can't even count on Grammy!

Mrs. Goodman kept me in from recess. I didn't feel like jumping rope anyway. She

shut the door and sat down at the desk beside me.

"Tabitha, is anything wrong?"

I didn't look at her. "I guess I didn't sleep too well last night."

"Is everything okay at home?"

"Mrs. Goodman, do you know anything about old people? Don't they get Oldtimers' disease and go crazy?"

38

Mrs. Goodman smiled at me. "If you mean Alzheimer's, yes, some people get it when they get older, but it doesn't make them crazy. Mostly it affects their memory, and they get confused, even about people they know and little daily things. Why do you ask?"

"Well, Grammy was always just a regular grandmother before. You know what I mean?"

"I've met your grandmother," she said. "She usually comes with your parents to open house. She seems pretty regular to me."

"Well, all of a sudden she wants to go to Mexico for Christmas. By herself! She wants to go and work at this place that hands out food and clothes to poor people. She always sends packages to them, but it's crazy to go down there. Isn't it?"

Mrs. Goodman thought for a long time. "Tabitha, I think we could all stand to be that crazy. If that's all that's going on with

39

your grandmother, I wouldn't fuss if I were you."

I sat for a while, but I couldn't make sense of anything.

Mrs. Goodman took my hand and said, "Are you having a problem with Kirsten again?"

I nodded. Mrs. Goodman is very familiar with the Queen and her court. But none of the teachers really know how awful she is, and they can only make her behave when they are around.

"Well," she said, "when people try to control you, you don't have to let them."

"What about when they tell lies about you?" I asked.

"Usually you just have to ignore them. Now, you can stay in and read if you want. I've got library duty."

Mrs. Goodman left me in my misery.

I opened my book, but of course I couldn't read.

So I closed it again, and I closed my

40

eyes. "Jesus, please get me out of this! I don't know what to do!"

If Jesus had a plan to get me out of that mess, He sure didn't put it into operation immediately. The rest of the day wasn't any better. At lunch I heard more versions of the same lie.

I heard that Kirsten's grandfather caught me and the man and held us till the police got there. I heard that Kirsten's grandfather is really an undercover policeman who knows all the druggies. I heard that I tried to sell drugs to Kirsten's grandfather, and that's how he caught me.

I tried Mrs. Goodman's advice—just ignore it.

After school Sara grabbed me as I was getting on my bus. "Kirsten says her grandfather said the guy was so stoned he couldn't stand up straight. Please tell me what happened. I promise I won't tell."

I shoved her away and got on the bus.

41

I do know why that man couldn't stand up straight. It wasn't from drugs. It was from Sonya's elbow! But no way was I telling anything. Ever!

42

·4·

The Dealer

I saw one of my tears drop into my tea as I was stirring it. Now in addition to a horrible life, I'd also have gross tea.

I sniffed and Grammy handed me a tissue. "Can you tell me what's the matter?"

I blew my nose. "Grammy, it's just horrible. The whole school is in a fit over something they don't know anything about. And it's all Kirsten's fault! Now they're saying I got arrested for drugs."

Grammy didn't say anything.

"Kirsten's grandfather has something to do with the fair, and he must have told her something about that man. But it's all wrong, and none of it makes sense, and no one talks about anything except me and my crimes!"

"Does your teacher know?" Grammy asked.

"She knows that the Queen is at war, but that's nothing new. The playground ladies make sure that no one is fighting, but they can't hear everything that everyone is saying. Besides, Kirsten is really sweet around grown-ups. It's enough to make you sick."

Grammy hugged me. "Maybe that's the problem. Maybe you're getting sick, honey. You really don't look so chipper."

"Oh Gram, it's just all this stuff at school. It takes me a year to get to sleep at night."

"Do you have bad dreams, Tabitha?"

"Well, it's never anything I can figure out, but it's always noisy, dark, scary stuff."

"Would it help if you slept in my room for a while?" Grammy asked me.

44

"Could I, Gram?" I started to cry again.

That night I slept a little better, and the next day was Friday. Mrs. Goodman handed out reminders that our school pictures would be taken on Monday.

Maybe life wasn't so bad after all. I figured that until school pictures were over and done with, the only thing on Kirsten's mind would be Kirsten and I would get a break.

I was right.

"Mom, Grammy, you guys aren't going to believe this! The Queen arrived for her royal portrait session with makeup on. Makeup! Of course her court fluttered around and told her how great she looked so they could borrow her blush.

"You would have loved watching her decide who could use it and who couldn't. She was just making sure that no one had a shot at looking better than she did."

Mom chuckled. "I wish I could watch all those mothers when the school pictures

45

come back and their kids are decorated with Wild Rose."

"Oh, Mom it wasn't like your blush. It was called Screamin' Peach. Kirsten had matching lipstick, but she wouldn't let anyone use it 'cause of germs."

"Smart girl."

"Even Sara and Kelly kept missing at jump rope because they were trying to see what was going on with the Queen. But at least everyone was making such a fuss over her, that for once no one fussed about me."

The photographer didn't make a fuss over anybody though, blush or no blush. In fact, he looked like he needed a week in the mountains. I can't imagine saying, "Next. Smile. Okay," over and over again all day, every day of my life. What a job! At least he didn't pop little bunnies in our faces and act like a goof.

For an extra ten dollars, he would pull down one of his "designer" window shade backgrounds. You could choose whether you

46

wanted to look like you were outdoors under an orange oak tree, or at a snowy window, or whatever.

But you had to choose ahead of time and have it marked on your paper and paid for. You weren't allowed to stand there and decide or change your mind.

"Kirsten and her bunch chose the 'Optic Excitement' background. They think the colored streaks and sparkles will make them look like movie stars."

"Are you sorry you chose the plain background, Tabitha?" Grammy asked.

"No. Regular blue seems best to me. Regular everything would be nice for a while."

Anyway, how can it cost him ten dollars to pull down a window shade? Maybe his job isn't so bad after all. "Next. Smile. Okay. Ten bucks please."

So on Monday no one noticed me. At least I didn't notice anyone noticing me.

And Tuesday and most of Wednesday

47

were even better. A traveling dinosaur museum came to the school. They weren't real dinosaurs. Someone had made real-sized skeletons out of car parts from the junkyard.

Mrs. Goodman said that the museum people had spent most of the night unloading sections from big trucks and bolting them together. The dinosaurs practically filled the ball field that we share with the junior high.

On Tuesday we had a program that was partly about recycling junk, partly about welding, and partly about dinosaurs.

They told us a million times not to climb on the dinosaurs, but at recess Willie MacIntosh climbed up the Rex and rode him like a bucking bronco. I thought Mrs. Samuels was going to have a heart attack! Willie has to stay in from recess for five days and sit in the principal's office.

Wednesday, Mrs. Goodman took us out to watch them take down the dinosaurs.

48

The junior high P.E. classes were helping. They couldn't play soccer anyway, because the field was covered with skeletons. I was just standing there watching when I heard a voice behind me.

"Are you Tabitha?"

I whirled around. I was facing a girl from the P.E. class. She was shaking, I thought from the cold, but she was also sweating.

Even her hair was a wreck and wet around her face.

"Look," she whispered, "I need something to pick me up. I feel awful and I can't stand it."

I backed away. "I don't know what you're talking about."

The girl was breathing hard. "You gotta help me. Mike said you were cool. He said you'd help me out."

"Well, he was wrong. I don't have anything, and I don't know anything."

"Well," she snarled, "you better not say anything, either. Get away from me and shut your trap."

I ran over and stood close to Mrs. Goodman. The girl was gone.

Later I told Grammy. She didn't say anything. She just stirred her tea and let me talk.

"So, now it's not just the kids in my

class. I mean I don't even know who this girl is! She really looked sick. Why would she talk to me like that, unless she thought I was a drug dealer?"

"Looks to me like your ship is taking on water fast, Tabitha."

"What?"

Grammy got up and rummaged around in the freezer until she came up with a package of Girl Scout cookies.

"Good for you, Gram. I didn't know we still had those."

Grammy opened the package and grinned. "If you had known they were here, they wouldn't be here, would they?"

"Probably not. But what did you mean about my ship, Gram?"

"Well, have you ever heard the saying, 'A slip of the lip can sink a ship'?"

I had my mouth full of cookies, so I just waited for her to go on.

"I think that expression probably came from a war, when someone might talk

51

without meaning to about battle plans, or secret positions of ships. Then a whole ship and all her crew could be lost because of one person's careless word."

Grammy touched my hand. "Your words didn't seem to have such terrible consequences at first. But now it looks to me like your poor little ship is in trouble."

Tied Up in Knots

Grammy made tacos for supper, my favorite. I ate two because I brought most of my lunch home again. I just can't seem to eat at school.

We all decided at supper that we'd spend the evening working on things to send to Mexico. I was still hoping to send them in the mail, and not in my grammy's suitcase.

Mom showed us her little dresses.

"They're all about a size four," she said. "But a smaller girl could wear them. And they've got a wide hem, so they can be let down."

"Mom, they're so sweet!" I held up a tiny

red plaid dress with a white collar. "I can just imagine a little black-haired Mexican girl wearing this. Too bad we can't see who gets it."

"That's one of the reasons I want to go," Grammy said quietly. "I've always just sent packages to an address. But once I see the people, I think it will be different."

Daddy looked up from picking through the scrap bag. "Did you hear any more details about the trip?"

Gram shook her head. "No, but as soon as I do, I'll let you know."

Daddy found a piece of the red plaid fabric. "Tabitha, will you show me how to make those dolls? Maybe we can make one to match each dress."

Mom looked over. "That's a great idea, Richard. I'll put a little button-down pocket on each dress to put the doll in."

"Wait, Daddy," I laughed. "I wouldn't want a doll with a red plaid face. Mom, is there anything here we could use for skin?"

We found some unbleached muslin in Mom's supply cabinet. But Daddy held up a piece of cotton cloth that reminded me of the color of coffee with cream.

"What about this, honey? It's darker than your skin, but it will look a little more like a Mexican than the muslin will."

"Do all Mexicans have dark skin?" I asked Grammy.

"I don't know. People usually come in all shades, no matter where they live. But," she laughed, "I doubt there are people anywhere with red plaid skin!"

We decided to make some from the muslin and the brown.

Deciding was easier than making.

Daddy and I sat there on the floor, surrounded by a pile of scraps. "Now what?" Daddy asked.

I didn't have any idea. "Our book didn't say how to make them. It only showed a picture of one. It just had a lump for the head."

55

So we experimented for a while and came up with some pretty weird-looking creations.

But Daddy would not give up. "Let's see. Suppose we just take a big square, and stuff some of these little scraps in the center of it. There, now we can tie something around the neck."

It wasn't bad really. Just a little too big

for a head. We took some of the scraps out of the lump and made it smaller.

"You know what, Dad? If we tie the neck with a really long piece, it'll look like two arms sticking out."

Mom and Grammy were trying to keep from laughing, but we heard them anyway.

Daddy pretended he was insulted. "Will you two please tend to your own business over there? We have everything under control. Someday these things will be as famous as Barbie dolls; then you'll be sorry."

Mom spoke very seriously. "Would you please make a pink camper to go with each one?"

"As you wish, Madam," he said. "You just concentrate on making the pocket big enough to hold it."

Mom threw a sofa pillow at the back of his head, but she missed by a mile.

Daddy picked it up. "Excuse me, Madam. I believe your pillow got away from you."

He flipped it back over his head without even looking, and it landed in her lap.

Daddy and I went back to work and tried to ignore them.

To make the hands, we tied knots on the ends of the arm pieces. Not bad. Just really long.

Before bedtime, we got a doll made that was small enough to fit in a little pocket, and had a regular-sized head and arms to match.

Daddy scooped up the scraps. "I think we'd better work on this a little each evening. The dresses should be pretty easy. We can just slip a square over their heads like a poncho, and tie it on with the apron."

"Dad, they don't have any shoulders. How will their dresses stay on?"

He looked totally blank for a minute; then he turned and popped the scrap bag into Mom's cabinet. "I don't know. Think about it. And sleep on it. We'll figure something out."

58

I thought about it, but I didn't sleep on it. I didn't sleep at all till Grammy came in. Then my dark, noisy dreams got her up twice before morning.

She sang to me a little bit to help me settle down again. Then she talked to me about the little dresses and the dolls.

"Just think," she said, "maybe I'll get to see who gets our dresses. But even if I don't, I'll get to be there and be a part of it. I've always been fascinated by people in other parts of the world. I think I'm going to learn how to say 'Jesus loves you' in Spanish."

I went to sleep again after that. The next time I woke up, I had been dreaming I was tangled up in red plaid material and I couldn't get away. And as always, there were flashing lights and clanging bells and loud, loud noises.

Proof Positive

The dinosaurs were gone from the school-yard the next morning. Unfortunately, Kirsten was still there.

She wouldn't talk to me though, even to say something mean. She acted like I had some kind of contagious disease. In fact, no one would talk to me. Every time I looked up, kids were looking at me, but they would always turn away.

My lunch wasn't very appetizing, but I ate some of it anyway. I couldn't count on Grammy for tacos two nights in a row.

Robbie somebody from Mrs. Samuels's class slid into the seat beside me while I

was stirring my applesauce.

He leaned a little bit my way, and whispered, "Meet us out by the jungle gym."

Then he disappeared, before I really even understood what he said.

Meet them at the jungle gym? Fat chance. I didn't know Robbie's last name, but I knew his reputation. I also knew that the gang he ran around with was mostly older kids and mostly bad news.

Anyway, I haven't been near that jungle gym in years. No one has unless they want trouble. All the teachers and playground ladies think it's great that the bigger boys are so interested in climbing and "being active."

The truth is that they have claimed the jungle gym as private property. No one goes there without their permission. And no one with any brains even wants to.

So there I was with an invitation.

Kelly leaned across the table. "What did he want, Tabitha?"

She and Sara were staring at me.

I was still staring at Robbie, who was halfway across the cafeteria by then. I shook my head. "Nothing. He didn't want anything. I don't even know him."

"Then why did he come over here?" Sara asked. "My sister says to stay away from him."

They got up to go outside.

"I'll be out in a minute," I called after them. "I want to try to break the record for my left foot today."

"Yeah, sure," Kelly mumbled.

The more I stirred that stupid applesauce, the angrier I got. This was all Kirsten's fault.

Outside, I couldn't find Sara and Kelly anywhere. Finally I spotted them sitting on the swings. When they saw me coming, they both got up and got in line for tetherball.

The Queen was watching the whole process with a smirk on her face.

My face was hot and I felt like hitting her. I marched right up to her.

"Kirsten, you think you're the queen of the world," I sputtered. "Well, I wish you'd tell your loyal subjects to back off and leave me alone. Because of your big mouth, I've got people I don't even know thinking I'm some kind of drug dealer. Just shut up and leave me alone."

Kirsten smiled an innocent-looking

64

smile. "Tabitha, you must be drunk or something. I don't even know what you're talking about."

"You know what I'm talking about."

The playground lady came over.

"What seems to be the problem here?" she asked.

It was amazing, but Kirsten actually had tears in her eyes. "I don't know," she whimpered. "I was just standing here and she came over and started yelling at me." All the queenlets nodded and agreed.

The playground lady took me by the arm.

Kirsten turned to her group. "See? I told you that would happen. She's in such bad shape she can't even control herself. She needs to get some help."

I pulled away from the playground lady and flew at Kirsten. "I don't need help!" I screamed. "Do you hear me? You got it all wrong! I don't need help. I don't. I don't, and especially not from you!" I burst into sobbing tears and ran into the woods behind the swings.

Maybe it was a slip of my own lip that started this whole business, but it was Kirsten's and Jason's and everyone else's big mouths that were chipping away at the hole in my ship.

While we were lining up to go in, I asked Sara what was going on with her and Kelly.

"We can't jump with you anymore."

"Why not?"

"Well, you know, because we don't want people to think . . ."

"Think what?"

"Well," Kelly said, "everyone says that you . . . well, you're getting a bad reputation, Tabitha. But Kirsten says you can't help it, 'cause of your family and all."

"My family?"

"Yeah," Sara said, "sorry. Our moms don't want us hanging around with people who might get us in trouble."

66

Kirsten came up behind me. "Tabitha, we all saw the bruise on your face the first day of school. You can't deny that. Maybe it's not your fault, but we can't let you get us in trouble too."

We went inside. What did my skateboard accident have to do with jumping rope? And how could it get them in trouble?

I decided to put Mrs. Goodman's advice to good use here. I'd have to ignore this. I couldn't make any sense of anything anymore.

Sara and Kelly didn't come to music with the rest of us. Mrs. Goodman brought them to the music room about fifteen minutes later. She apologized to the music teacher and left. But Kelly was sitting where I could see her. Every time I looked over she was staring at me. She was just about in tears.

Then after class she practically killed

67

herself to get in line where she wouldn't have to be near me.

What a weird life I have. Everyone looks at me until I look at them. Everyone talks about me, but no one will talk to me. I feel like I've got some awful disease they're afraid of catching.

Unless stupidity is a disease, they aren't in any danger.

Jason's Big Mouth

Mrs. Goodman told us to get out our books for silent reading. Then she said, "Tabitha, would you please come with me?"

A buzz went through the room. Kirsten said out loud, "It's about time. Maybe now she'll get some help."

Mrs. Goodman reached over to the front of her desk and turned on the tape recorder. She always does that when she leaves the room. "This is a blank tape," she told us at the beginning of the year. "And it's going to stay blank. I don't ever want to hear anyone's voice on this tape."

The class got quiet immediately, and she

and I went out into the hall.

"Tabitha, I'm quite concerned over things I've been hearing about you. Would you like a chance to tell your side of the story?"

"That's just it, Mrs. Goodman. There isn't any story. I didn't do anything."

"Well, what do they think you did?"

"They think I'm a druggie or an alcoholic or a shoplifter or I don't know what else. They won't talk to me anymore. Even Sara and Kelly won't jump rope with me."

Mrs. Goodman nodded. "How did all this get started?"

I shrugged.

My teacher put her arm around my shoulders. "How are things with your grandmother? Is she still going to Mexico?"

"I think so. Grammy's about the only friend I have left, and she won't be here for Christmas, and I can't get to sleep at night, so I have to sleep in her room, but even that doesn't really help."

"You had a big sore under your chin on the first day of school. How did that happen?"

"It happened on Jason's skateboard ramp." Didn't she remember? Everybody asked about it, even though it was almost healed up. I must have told it fifty times.

"Was Jason there when it happened?"

I nodded. What did all this have to do with anything?

"Tabitha, I care about you. I want you to tell me if someone is hurting you or doing something to you that you don't like, and I'll try to help you."

"Kirsten."

"Kirsten? What is she doing?"

"She's spreading lies about me."

"Tabitha, if gossip doesn't have any truth in it, it will usually go away after a while. Did you try just ignoring her?"

I started to cry. Mrs. Goodman wanted to help, but she just didn't understand.

She handed me a tissue. "Sara and Kelly still want to be your friends. In fact they

71

are very worried about you. They don't think you are safe at home, and they're afraid you're getting mixed up with a bad bunch of kids."

I stared at Mrs. Goodman, but I could hardly see her through my tears. Not safe at home? That's the only place I have any peace at all! And mixed up with what bunch of kids?

It was all too much. I couldn't stop crying, so Mrs. Goodman said I could go to the nurse's room and lie down.

I sat on the bus waiting for the older kids to load.

Jeannie Carter got on. She is a cheer-leader, just about the smartest kid in the junior high, and she doesn't belong on this bus.

She stopped to talk to the driver. "I'm going home with Karen. I've got a note." She handed him a piece of paper.

He mumbled something and motioned her on. Driving a school bus is probably another great job to have. I'll put it on my list of career opportunities.

Jeannie came down the aisle, but she didn't sit with Karen. She sat with me!

I didn't really look at her or anything. But when the bus started out, she moved a little closer to me.

"Your name's Tabitha, right?"

"Yeah."

"Look," she said, "I don't know what's going on with you. But I hear stuff, you know? If you need some help, or you want someone to talk to, these people are cool."

She handed me a little card with an 800 number on it. It said,

"TeenFree"
Confidential Help
for Chemical Dependency
Call Us—We Care

73

"Really," she said, "don't be afraid to call them. You don't have to give your name or anything. They helped me. I've been free for more than two years."

Then she slid farther down the aisle to where Karen was waiting.

I just shoved the card in my pocket. There sure were a bunch of people willing to help. Too bad I didn't have a problem.

74

But later that afternoon the problem I didn't have got worse. And this time it was Jason's mouth, not mine, that caused it.

Jason and I were on my porch getting my skateboard and stuff, and we were just about to leave for his house.

A car pulled into our driveway.

I recognized the man who came up the steps.

"Hello, Tabitha."

It was the sergeant who had talked to us at the police station.

Grammy came to the door. "Hi. What can we do for you?"

The man pulled his ID out of his jacket pocket and showed it to Grammy. "Are the Bigbees in, Ma'am? I just want to talk to them and to Tabitha for a minute."

Mom appeared behind Grammy. "Sergeant Ryder?" she asked. "Hello, come in." Then she noticed Jason.

"Jason, why don't you run on home. Tabitha will be along in a minute. Okay?"

Jason left, but not without an eyeful of the policeman and his badge.

8

The Sinking Ship

Saturday morning was bright and warm, just like summer. I wanted to go down to Jason's skateboard ramp, but I wasn't sure he'd want me.

I wasn't sure I wanted him, either. Not after yesterday. He had been so impressed with the policeman at my door that he just couldn't resist spreading the news.

I wish just one person had come up to me and said, "Hey, Tabitha, I hear there was a policeman at your house."

But nobody did.

All day long they whispered to each other where they thought I couldn't hear them. They actually expected the cops to bust into the classroom and haul me away in handcuffs!

Boy, would they be disappointed if they knew the truth. Sergeant Ryder just came to tell us it was all over. We won't have to go to the trial because the guy confessed, and we don't have to worry about him anymore.

Right. I don't have to worry. All I have to do is go to school.

At least I didn't have to go to school today. I went out to tend to Androcles.

"You poor old bunny. You haven't gotten much attention this week, have you? Do you miss your babies?"

Androcles snuggled into my arms and bumped her head up against my hand. She wanted me to scratch between her ears.

"I feel just like you, Androcles—a lonely bunny in a whole yard full of noisy, nosy chickens."

I scratched her some more and set her

78

down on the ground. She hopped right into the middle of a circle of chickens, sent them flying, and grabbed whatever they had been fussing over.

"Way to go, girl. That's the way to show them!"

Mom came over to the chicken yard. "Tabitha, Mrs. Goodman just phoned. She's on her way out to see us."

It took me a second to answer. "My teacher? She's coming here? To our house?"

Mom nodded. "She sounded worried. Is everything okay at school?"

Everything was not okay at school. "I didn't do anything wrong, Mom. I'm not in trouble, am I?"

"She didn't say. She just wanted to know if Daddy were home too, and asked if we could talk."

Daddy was home, all right. While we were waiting for the teacher to show up, I couldn't tell if he was angry, or worried, or if he thought the whole thing was funny. His face kept changing.

But Grammy knew what to do. She made a pot of tea and a pan of shortbread cookies.

Mrs. Goodman finally pulled into the driveway. It sure is strange to have your teacher at your house. She kept talking about how nice the day was and how warm it was for this time of year.

We all sat around the kitchen table, and everyone had tea. (Do you take sugar or honey? Just plain, thanks.) Mrs. Goodman thought the cookies were lovely. (They're made with real butter, aren't they?) Then there was just weird silence.

Mom finally took charge. "Mrs. Goodman, do you want Tabitha to stay and hear what you have to say?"

"Oh, yes. And you too," she said to Grammy. "We need as much input here as possible."

Input? What I need is a transfer to another school.

Mom let out a long breath. "Then please tell us what brought you out here. We're all a little confused."

My teacher blushed. "I know, I'm sorry. The problem is that I'm confused too.

"There's something going on at school that no one can figure out. So I decided to get to the bottom of it. Apparently there are rumors flying about that Tabitha is

81

involved in drugs and in trouble with the police."

Daddy almost laughed, but he caught himself in time. "You're serious, aren't you?"

Mrs. Goodman shrugged her shoulders. "That's just it. I can't tell because no one can tell me anything definite, not even Tabitha. So I advised her to just ignore what people are saying.

"But she seems so stressed; I'm sure you've noticed. And then Sara and Kelly came to me wondering if I could get some help for Tabitha. They said they were afraid she wasn't safe at home, and that's why she was getting into drugs."

Daddy straightened up and scowled. "That's ridiculous!"

Mrs. Goodman's shoulder's sagged, and she pushed her tea cup back. She leaned on her elbows and rubbed her eyes with both hands.

"I know it is, but I'd like to clear this up

before it goes any further. It doesn't take much more than rumors to start a child abuse investigation."

Grammy spoke up. "Tabitha has been under considerable stress, but I don't think it's drug related. Seems to me it's gossip related."

Mrs. Goodman nodded. "If I could just figure out how all this got started."

Everyone was very quiet for a minute, so I guess I startled them when I spoke. "I started it."

They all looked at me.

"I started it when I told them I'd been at the police station. When I wouldn't tell them any more, they made stuff up."

Mrs. Goodman looked at Mom and Daddy. "What happened?"

Daddy sighed. "Just before school started, Tabitha was at the fair where she almost got abducted."

Abducted! I'd heard that word at the police station. It means the same as kid-

83

napped, but it sounds so horrible.

"She didn't get hurt," Mom said. "She managed to get away, and the man is in jail now. But I'm afraid it's not over for Tabitha. She hasn't really dealt with it yet."

Mom knew more than I thought she did. You can bet I'm not over it. I think about it every minute. My ship really is sinking and I'm trapped inside. Now it looks like my whole family is going down with me.

I was almost ready to cry. My teacher reached over and put her hand on mine.

"I'm so sorry that happened to you Tabitha, and I'm glad they've caught the guy. No one at school understands what you've been through. If they did, they'd ease up I'm sure."

I shook my head. "I don't ever want to talk about it. It's too embarrassing."

Daddy made me look at him. "Honey, is it more embarrassing than the things

84

they've been making up?"

Mrs. Goodman tried again. "I told you to ignore this, but I was wrong. The only thing that will fix this mess is a good dose of the truth.

"There's a famous saying," she went on. " 'You shall know the truth and the truth shall set you free.' "

She waited a minute and then said, "Tabitha, your classmates need to know the truth, and you all need to be set free from this awful gossip. My advice to you now is to tell them."

"What is the best way to do that?" Grammy asked.

Mrs. Goodman thought a minute. "You know, we have a safety talk last thing every Monday afternoon. Usually I just read something about first aid, or biking in traffic, or whatever I find."

Then she turned to me. "Tabitha, you could use that time on Monday. I believe it would help you get done with what

85

happened to you as well as quiet things down at school."

Mom told Mrs. Goodman she'd call her later, and she and Daddy walked her out to her car.

When Daddy came back in, he sat down at the table again and took my hand. "I think we need to pray about this."

He closed his eyes. "Father, we need some help here. Please tell us what to do, and please help Tabitha feel safe again. We love her, and we love You. In Jesus' name, Amen."

A prayer like that just made me cry all the more. But Daddy held my hand till I stopped.

"Now, young lady," he said, "you have a decision to make. Are you going to give the safety talk to your class on Monday?"

"Daddy, what will I say?"

"Don't worry about what to say, honey. This isn't like a book report or anything. Just open up your heart and tell them what's there."

Grammy pulled her Bible off the top of the refrigerator. "Listen to this. It's from Matthew chapter ten. The disciples were going to be arrested for preaching.

"And Jesus tells them, 'Do not worry about what to say or how to say it. At that time you will be given what to say, for it will not be you speaking, but the Spirit of your Father speaking through you.' "

Grammy closed her Bible and gave me a hug. "God will give you the right words when the time comes. You just get up there, open your heart, and see what comes out."

Of course, it was impossible to get to sleep that night. Grammy never stirred. It was nice to have her nearby, but there was too much to think about.

I finally decided to get up and go get something to eat.

I closed Grammy's door when I left so I wouldn't wake her up turning on the lights.

But the lights were already on in the kitchen. Daddy was in there pulling pieces

87

of meat off the leftover chicken and dipping them in tartar sauce.

He looked up. "You caught me! Do you want some?"

I sat down, took a piece of white meat and salted it. He could have the tartar sauce.

"Can't sleep?" he asked.

I shook my head.

"Tabitha, do you know that God doesn't expect you to be strong? In fact, He would rather you weren't!"

"That's good," I told him. "There's no way I'm strong enough to tell the whole class. I think I'd better just quit school."

9

The Truth

Oh, great idea, Tabitha," Daddy laughed. "Quitting school sounds like a good plan!"

"Well, I can't tell the class, and I can't not tell them. What am I supposed to do?"

Daddy smiled as he wiped some tartar sauce off the table and slid Grammy's Bible over closer to me.

"See here. I was reading in II Corinthians. 'My grace is sufficient for you, for my power is made perfect in weakness.'"

"What does that mean?"

"It means that if we were all strong and powerful, we'd run around bragging about

89

how great we are and have no time for God.

"He'd rather we admitted we were weak, and let Him be strong for us. Then when it's over, we can brag about what the Lord did for us, instead of what we did."

I let out my breath. "Sounds easy."

But Daddy shook his head. "Actually, honey, it's hard, especially for grown-ups to do. But maybe you're still young enough to make it work."

I waited for him to explain.

"See, the Bible tells us in Ephesians six that we can use our faith as a shield to protect us from the fiery darts of the enemy. The only thing is, to use a shield, you have to face your enemy."

I was beginning to get it. "You mean face the class even if I think I can't?"

He nodded. "God's part is to give you the words to say and use them to settle these rumors. Your part is to face your class and have faith that God will do His part.

90

"Do you trust God, Tabitha? Do you think He's strong enough to protect you?"

I thought about that for a minute. "Yes, I do. He certainly protected me at the fair, even though I was stupid."

"Good," Daddy said. "Then do you think He's smart enough to know what words to use for your safety talk?"

"Yes, of course He is. No one's smarter than God."

"God's given you a way to get free, honey. All you have to do is trust Him and do it."

Daddy took a breath and looked at the chicken bones. "Well, I hope Grammy didn't have a plan for this chicken. There isn't much left." He started to wrap it up.

Then he tore off a little piece of aluminum foil and folded it.

"There." He handed it to me. "It's a little shield to keep in your pocket. It'll remind you to let God do His job."

When I went back to bed, I dreamt about

91

chickens walking around with jars of tartar sauce. Nothing noisy for once.

Monday morning, I was ready for school early, and I had the shield in my pocket. Grammy made me oatmeal with raisins. She even let me put brown sugar on it.

Grammy handed me my backpack and kissed the top of my head.

"This is a test for your faith, Tabitha. God doesn't get tired of getting you out of trouble. He wants to use your trouble to help you grow and become strong in Him. He'll be with you the whole time."

Mom hugged me and made me zip my sweatshirt. "We'll be praying for you, honey. And I'll pick you up after school so you don't have to take the bus home. We love you."

The whole day passed in kind of a fog. Mrs. Goodman didn't say anything about the math paper I handed in with only one problem done.

She also gave me a library pass to use during recess. I don't even remember lunch.

Toward the end of the day she announced, "Please hurry and get cleaned up. We want to save a little extra time for our safety talk today. It's a special one."

When we were all back in our seats, she said, "Tabitha told me this morning that she would like to give the safety talk today. Now I know I usually do it, but she has something important she wants to say. Tabitha?"

I dragged myself to the front of the room and turned to face the class.

I looked at the floor. *Well, Jesus, You said You'd give me the words. Here goes.* I took a breath and opened my mouth. What came out didn't sound much like a safety talk.

"I'm not a criminal. I didn't really get arrested. And I'm not a liar either. I just

93

thought arrested meant you had to go to the police station."

The kids started to snicker and move around. Mrs. Goodman spoke out sharply. "Quiet!"

By the time they settled down again, I was so weak I wanted to cry.

I stuffed my hands in my pockets and felt the crinkle of aluminum foil. It was the shield Daddy made for me. I remembered about my faith putting out the fiery darts. But I had to face the enemy, right?

I started in again.

"I'm not a shoplifter. I'm not a druggie. I've never had anything to do with drugs at all. Or alcohol. I don't even know what beer tastes like, and I don't ever intend to find out."

The class was still shuffling around, but at least they didn't say anything.

"Also my family is really great and no one ever hurts me or messes with me."

I stopped and the class thought I was

94

done. Kirsten whispered loudly, "That doesn't sound like a safety talk to me!" But Mrs. Goodman came up behind the Queen and put a hand on her shoulder.

Then she said softly, "Please go on Tabitha. There will be no more interruptions."

I took a deep breath, and held on to my little shield so tightly I squashed it.

"But while I was at the fair, I did something really stupid that almost got me kidnapped or even killed."

There was a big gasp from everyone. I couldn't stop now. If the truth was going to set me free, it'd better hurry. I felt like my heart was going to explode.

I told them about the plan that Sonya and I had. I left her name out of it, and I made it clear she didn't go to this school. Otherwise they wouldn't have been satisfied until they found out who she was.

"We met this man who seemed really nice at first. We never suspected anything. I mean he was great. Just like somebody's brother, or father or something. We never once felt nervous or scared."

Then I told them how he suddenly changed and how he trapped us so we couldn't get away.

"The fair is so loud." I stopped for a second and felt the shield in my pocket. "It's just . . . it's just so awfully loud. There's so much confusion. We were too

96

scared to scream, but no one would have heard us even if we had. People were crowded everywhere, but no one knew we needed help."

I explained how we fought back, and got away and about all the questions at the police station and everything. I told them why the policeman came to our house.

I talked fast to get it over with, but I told them everything.

"So my safety talk is this: Don't ever think that Stranger Awareness stuff is just for babies. It's true. Don't talk to anyone you don't know, and don't go anywhere alone. If I had been by myself, I might be dead."

There didn't seem to be anything else to say. I noticed that Mrs. Goodman was crying and so were some of the girls. Not Kirsten, but she was staring at her desk.

I sat down and didn't look at anyone. Nobody moved. Mrs. Goodman told the class. "Silent reading please, till school's over."

She knelt down beside my desk. "Thank you, Tabitha. Your mom is waiting outside for you. You're excused."

I looked up at her and wiped my tears away. I picked up my backpack and sweatshirt and left.

10

Free Indeed

■ have to admit I was nervous about going back to school. Sometimes it's easier when you know they're going to hate you than when you don't have any idea how they're going to act.

But I'm happy to report that at last my life is regular again.

Sara and Kelly were waiting for me the next day when I got there.

Sara stood twisting the buttons on her sweater. "I'm really sorry I was such an idiot, Tabitha."

Kelly nodded. "Me too."

I knew what they meant, and I really wanted to get past everything that had happened and be friends again.

"Well, I'm an idiot too, you know, so we're even. Let's go try and set a new Red Hot Pepper record."

They both giggled and practically dragged me across the playground.

I guess everything will be quiet now until the next crisis. If Kirsten can't find a good one in a week or two, she won't let that stop her. She'll make one up.

But for now she's busy practicing cheers. She doesn't actually practice herself, of course. She stands facing her queenlets, watching them practice and giving them advice. She thinks that when she gets to junior high, she's going to be Queen Cheerleader, and pick the rest of the squad herself.

I actually hope she does get to be a cheerleader. It must be awful to have to threaten people to be your friends.

The other day Jason called and asked when I was coming down to use his ramp. I've decided my goal is to get good on my skateboard before the ramp is covered with snow. And now that the weather's getting colder we're wearing more clothes, which cuts down on the scrapes and bruises.

Grammy got her information from Mexico. She read it to us at supper.

"I have to get there by December 18, and it's over on the 23rd, so if I make my reservation right away, I can be sure to get home for Christmas."

"Can we do the baking before you go, Gram?"

"Absolutely. I'll only be gone about a week. That's not so bad."

Daddy smiled at her. "Well, you have my blessing, Mom. Go ahead and call tomorrow for a reservation. Most of the airlines charge less if you book ahead anyway. Get an exact price and we'll go down and pay them right away."

Grammy smiled. "There's just one more thing. It'll cost $155.00 for me to eat and sleep while I'm there. I should have enough in my savings by then. Just pray that the chickens lay like crazy, and everybody wants the eggs."

Mom took Grammy's hand. "We'll help you as much as we can," she said. "You just go and have a great time." Then she stopped herself. "Well, it doesn't sound like it will be fun exactly, but we understand how much this means to you."

Grammy squeezed her hand and said, "Thanks."

Then she turned to me. "What about you, Tabitha? Is it okay with you?"

"Well, I guess it is, if you'll promise to be back in time for Christmas."

Grammy laughed. "Tabitha, if that plane leaves for Maine on the 23rd, I'll be on it."

So Daddy and I had better get busy with our knot dolls. Mom's got seven dresses made already and we're lagging way behind.

Gram showed us a picture they had sent her of a school near where she was going. Most of the kids looked too young to go to school. Things must be different in Mexico.

Not all the kids had brown faces, but most of them did. And the ones who were smiling were *really* smiling. Not like our school pictures.

It was nice to think that some little girls like these would be wearing our dresses with the little knot dolls in the pockets (if Daddy and I get them done).

Grammy's lucky, really, to get to meet them.

And it turns out she doesn't have to count only on her egg money. Mr. Jepson, who is our friend from across the street, gave her fifty dollars as an early Christmas present. He said it was easier to wrap than an umbrella, which is what he gave her last year.

Grammy doesn't know it, but Mom's

going to ask the ladies' Sunday school class to take an offering. So my gram is going to Mexico, and it doesn't seem crazy at all.

I'm sleeping in my own room again, and actually sleeping, too! Sometimes the noisy dreams start, but Androcles always jumps into the middle of things and kicks until they quiet down. I'm probably the only person in the world who dreams about a protector rabbit.

I saved that TeenFree card that Jeannie Carter gave me. Every morning I've been waiting where the buses unload to see if I can find that girl from the P.E. class.

Yesterday I spotted her and ran to catch up.

Her eyes were shiny and kept jerking back and forth. I don't think she remembered me.

"Look," I said, "I don't know what's going on with you, but you asked me to help you. Here. If you really want help, these people are cool."

I handed her the little card.

She took it very slowly without looking at it, and put it in her jacket pocket.

"Please call them," I said. "You don't have to give your name or anything."

As I started to leave, I looked up and saw

Jeannie Carter watching us. "Hi, Tabitha. Hi, Erin," she said to the girl.

Jeannie put her arm around Erin's waist. Then she turned and winked at me.

Would you like to share Jesus' love with other people, like Tabitha's family did? If you would, you may write to the address below for more information about their organization, and how they help people in the United States, Mexico, and a number of other countries:

Calvary Commission
P.O. Box 412
Hidalgo, TX 78557

Or you may wish to talk to someone on the missions board or social concerns committee at your church. They may know of a specific family who needs help, or they may be aware of other ways you may contribute to the needy in your area.

Tabitha Sarah Bigbee has pickle stew . . .

. . . and Jason's not about to help.

When Tabitha and Jason put their two rabbits together, they didn't realize they'd end up with nine baby bunnies as well. Jason paid his half of the vet bill, but even though his rabbit is the father, he thinks his duty is done. Now Tabitha is faced with paying the rest of the vet bill and finding homes for nine baby bunnies. All she really wanted to do this summer was buy a skateboard!

Tabitha doesn't mean to get into trouble, but trouble seems to have a way of finding her. Good thing she has her Grammy, who continually reminds her of God's love and forgiveness, and a mom and dad who understand a lot.

by Wendy Lord

Chariot Books
David C. Cook Publishing Co.

Gorilla on the Midway

Tabitha Sarah Bigbee is spending a week at the fair . . .

. . . a week she'll never forget.

Tabitha and Sonya have entered their rabbits in the fair, so they're staying the whole week to take care of them. Grammy says this may be the answer to Tabitha's prayer to get to know Sonya better—and maybe even get her for a best friend. Things go fairly well for the two girls, until they meet the gorilla on the midway.

Tabitha doesn't mean to get into trouble, but trouble seems to have a way of finding her. Good thing she has her Grammy, who continually reminds her of God's love and forgiveness, and a mom and dad who understand a lot.

by Wendy Lord

Chariot Books™
David C. Cook Publishing Co.

Chocolate Chips and Trumpet Tricks

"Brussels Sprouts!"

Alex sure does love food—chocolate chips, apple turnovers, meat loaf, French fries—but the food she loves most is the food found in God's Word.

Come join Alex in these fun-filled devotions and discover, as she does, how feeding on God's Word can help your relationship with Him keep growing. Through her everyday adventures, you and Alex will see how God can give us the strength to do what is right, and that He still loves us even when we do what is wrong.

So get ready for a real meal, and jump into the fun with Alex.

by Nancy Simpson Levene

Chariot Books
David C. Cook Publishing Co.

It's Alex!

"Brussels Sprouts!"

Every kid gets into the predicaments Alex does—ones that start out small and mushroom. Whether it's figuring out how to replace lost shoelaces or trying to win a contest, you'll laugh along with Alex as she learns that God always loves her, no matter what she's done.

Be sure to read all the books in the Alex series:

Shoelaces and Brussels Sprouts
French Fry Forgiveness
Hot Chocolate Friendship
Peanut Butter and Jelly Secrets
Mint Cookie Miracles
Cherry Cola Champions
The Salty Scarecrow Solution
Peach Pit Popularity
T-Bone Trouble
Grapefruit Basket Upset
Apple Turnover Treasure
Crocodile Meatloaf

by Nancy Simpson Levene

Chariot Books
David C. Cook Publishing Co.